A Kooties Club MYSTERY

Membership Card

Name _____

Nickname _____

School _____

Age _____

The Mystery of the Too Crisp Cash

by M. J. Cosson

Perfection Learning® CA

Cover and Inside Illustrations: Michael A. Aspengren

For information, contact
Perfection Learning® Corporation,
1000 North Second Avenue, P.O. Box 500,
Logan, Iowa 51546-1099.
Paperback 0-7891-2298-7
Cover Craft® 0-7807-7270-9
8 9 10 PP 08 07 06 05 04 03

Table of Contents

Introduction

Abe, Ben, Gabe, Toby, and Ty live in a large city. There isn't much for kids to do. There isn't even a park close by.

Their neighborhood is made up of apartment houses and trailer parks. Gas stations and small shops stand where the parks and grass used to be. And there aren't many houses with big yards.

7

Ty and Abe live in an apartment complex. Next door is a large vacant lot. It is full of brush, weeds, and trash. A path runs across the lot. On the other side is a trailer park. Ben and Toby live there.

Across the street from the trailer park is a big gray house. Gabe lives in the top apartment of the house.

The five boys have known each other since they started school. But they haven't always been friends.

The other kids say the boys have cooties. And the other kids won't touch them with a ten-foot pole. So Abe, Ben, Gabe, Toby, and Ty have formed their own club. They call it the Kooties Club.

Here's how to join. If no one else will have anything to do with you, you're in.

The boys call themselves the Koots for short. Ben's grandma calls his grandpa an *old coot*. And Ben thinks his grandpa is pretty cool. So if he's an old coot, Ben and his friends must be young koots.

The Koots play ball and hang out with each other. But most of all, they look for mysteries to solve.

Chapter 1

Who's the Boss?

Toby sat in front of the TV. He was watching a talk show.

Toby's mom wasn't home from work yet. So she didn't know what Toby was watching. She made him watch PBS when she was home.

The front door opened. Toby's older brother Todd walked in. "Turn

that off," he ordered. "Mom doesn't want you to watch that junk."

"Make me," replied Toby.

"Okay," said Todd. "I will!"

He walked slowly toward Toby. Todd held his arms in front of him. He opened his fingers wide. A mean grin crossed Todd's face. He acted like he wanted to grab Toby by the throat.

Toby ducked and ran down the hall. He screamed.

Todd ran after him. He grabbed Toby by the back of his shirt. He pulled Toby to the floor. Then Todd jumped on top of him.

"Ow!" yelled Toby.

"Who's the boss, runt?" asked Todd.

"You are!" cried Toby.

11

"Right," said Todd. "And don't you ever forget it! And this boss has a job for you. Go to the Stop 'n Shop. Get me the new Super Guy comic book."

Toby was flat on his back. Todd sat on top of him, looking down into his face. There wasn't much Toby could do. He had to agree. Oh well. It would give him something to do.

"All right," said Toby.

Todd pulled Toby to his feet. Then he reached into his pocket.

"Here's a twenty," Todd said. "Don't lose it. I worked hard for it. And bring back all the change," he added.

Then Todd grinned at his younger brother. "Well, go ahead and buy

yourself a candy bar. Buy me one too." He told Toby what he wanted.

Toby stuffed the money into his pocket. He ran out the door.

Toby had to walk past Ben's trailer on the way to the Stop 'n Shop. Ben was sitting on the step.

"I've got money!" Toby said. "I can buy a candy bar. Want half?"

"Sure!" Ben jumped up and joined Toby. They walked down the block to the Stop 'n Shop.

13

Chapter 2

Caught in the Act

This seemed to be the boys' lucky day. At the store, they found the comic book Todd wanted. But best of all, Ben found some candy on sale. They were two for the price of one.

The boys carried the items to the counter. Toby handed the clerk the twenty-dollar bill.

The clerk took the money and rang up the sale. He started to put the bill in the cash drawer. But he stopped.

He held the bill up to the light. He
frowned. Then he turned and looked
at Ben and Toby.

"Where did you boys get this money?" he asked.

"From my brother," said Toby.

"Well, it's no good," the clerk told the boys. "It's fake. You boys stay right here. I'm going to call the cops."

Ben's and Toby's mouths dropped open. They backed toward the door.

"I told you boys to stay put," said the clerk. He turned and made the phone call.

When he hung up, he said, "Somebody will be here in just a minute. You boys sit down over there." He pointed to the back corner of the store. There was no way to escape.

Toby and Ben sat down.

"What do you think they'll do to us? Will they use handcuffs?" whispered Ben.

16

"They may take us to the station," said Toby. "I wonder if they will put us in jail."

"Just tell them your brother gave you the money," said Ben. "He's the one who should go to jail."

After several minutes, a police officer walked in the door. He carried a pen and a clipboard.

The officer walked over to the clerk. The clerk handed him the money. He whispered something to the officer. Then he pointed to the boys.

The officer frowned. He clipped the bill to the clipboard. Then he turned and walked toward Ben and Toby.

17

Chapter 3

A Mystery!

"Hello, kids. I'm Officer Gomez. What are your names?" he asked. He wrote down their names. "I need to talk with your parents," he said.

Ben and Toby got into the police car. The officer drove down the street to the trailer court. They went to Toby's trailer first.

Todd answered the door. He looked at the policeman. Then he

looked at Toby and Ben. "What's going on?" he asked.

"That's just what I want to know," said Officer Gomez. "Are your parents here? I'd like to talk with them."

"Our mom's at work," said Todd. "What's wrong? What did they do?" He continued to stare at Toby and Ben.

"These boys tried to pass some fake money. It's a bad crime," said the policeman.

The officer took the twenty-dollar bill from the clipboard. He showed it to Todd.

"How do you know it's fake?" asked Todd.

The officer held the bill so all three boys could see it.

"See," he said. "The color is a little too green. And the paper is too crisp. It looks and feels like new money.

"Most people who pass fake money try to make it look worn. They wrinkle it and press it with their hands. They want it to look old and dirty."

Officer Gomez continued. "The art is very good. It's probably a photocopy of a real twenty."

Todd's mouth dropped open. "But that's my money! Ms. Ngu just paid me to mow her lawn. I got that money less than an hour ago."

"It's yours? Then why did you send your brother to spend it?" asked the officer.

Todd's face grew red. He looked down. "I didn't want anybody to see me buying a comic book," he said.

Officer Gomez laughed. "Too big for that kid stuff, huh?"

21

Toby smiled. He made a note to himself. He had something on Todd. Now he could get even with his brother.

Toby formed a plan in his mind. Just wait till the next time he saw Todd with a girl. Toby would ask Todd how he liked his latest Super Guy comic book. That should get him!

Toby looked up at the officer. He was asking Todd, "Where does Ms. Ngu live?"

"A few blocks from here," said Todd. "I don't know the address. But I can show you the house."

"When will your mother be home?" asked Officer Gomez.

"In about half an hour," said Todd.

22

"Okay, I'll come back later," said the officer. "Be ready to go visit Ms. Ngu."

Officer Gomez got into his car.

Toby asked Todd, "Can we go with you to Ms. Ngu's?"

"Are you kidding?" said Todd. "Mom won't let you. And I don't think the cop will either."

Todd went back inside. Ben and Toby stayed outside. They looked at each other. They were thinking the same thing. A mystery!

"We have to get the other Koots," said Toby.

Chapter 4

The Koots' Plan

A few minutes later, the Koots were sitting on Toby's steps.

"We have to spy on Todd," said Toby. "We have to find out where Ms. Ngu lives. Maybe we can watch her get arrested! Maybe we'll see them take out the copier she uses to make the money."

24

"How will we get to Ms. Ngu's?" asked Gabe. "We can't run as fast as the police car."

"No kidding!" said Toby.

"I know!" said Ben. "We can look for her address in the phone book. Then we can get there and hide before Todd and the cops come."

"Great idea!" said Ty. "Go get your phone book, Toby."

Toby got the phone book. "How do you spell Ngu?" he asked.

"N," everybody said at once. Toby found the names starting with N.

"U," said Ben. Toby looked up Nu. That wasn't it.

"Try N-y-o-u. Nyou," said Gabe. "That's how it sounds." That wasn't it either.

"Try N-e-w. New," suggested Ty. That wasn't right.

"Maybe it's K-n-e-w. Like I *knew* the answer," offered Abe. Nothing.

"Maybe it's like that animal, g-n-u. You say it like *new*. Try G," said Ben. No luck.

"I know!" said Toby. "I bet it's like Nguyen's Bakery. It's Ng something."

Toby looked up Ng, and there was just one Ngu. It was 122 Baker Street. And it was only two blocks away.

"Wow!" said Gabe. "It's spelled just like Nguyen's Bakery. And it's on Baker Street! Is that weird or what?"

"Let's go!" said Toby.

The Koots were on their way to Baker Street.

Chapter 5

A Dead End

When the Koots got to Baker Street, they found the house. The numbers above the door read 122.

"I know this is the right house," said Toby.

"I thought you didn't know where Ms. Ngu lived. How can you tell?" asked Abe.

"I can tell it's the right house because the grass has just been cut," said Toby.

"Good eye, Sherlock," said Ty. "Look, we can hide in these bushes," Ty added. Each boy found a spot where he could hide but still see the house.

Soon a car stopped in front of 122 Baker Street. A woman was with Todd. She had on a suit instead of a uniform. She didn't look much like a police officer.

The woman and Todd walked up the sidewalk. They rang the doorbell. A lady came to the door.

"I can't hear," whispered Gabe. "I need to get closer. You guys stay here."

Gabe ducked down. He ran across the yard of the house next door. He kept low behind the bushes. Then he ran behind the house.

28

The Koots next saw Gabe inching
along the side of Ms. Ngu's house. He
was right around the corner from the
front door. His back was pressed to
the side of the house.

"I hope they don't see him,"
whispered Ben.

The Koots watched the officer pull something from her purse. She held it out to Ms. Ngu. It was the twenty-dollar bill in a plastic bag.

Ms. Ngu turned and went inside the house. She came back out with another bill. The three looked at the two bills. Ms. Ngu shook her head.

They talked some more. Ms. Ngu pointed down the street. Then Todd and the officer left. Ms. Ngu went inside her house.

Gabe inched back around the house. He ran back to the bushes. The rest of the Koots asked at once, "What did they say?"

Gabe sat down on the grass. The other Koots joined him.

"They looked at both bills," Gabe began. "Ms. Ngu said she got one of the bills at the gas station. The other twenty came from the cash machine. That was at the bank.

"The cop said the bank would spot that funny money," he continued. "She thinks the funny twenty came from the gas station."

"Which gas station?" the Koots asked at the same time.

"The one at the end of my street!" answered Gabe.

"Let's go!" shouted Toby.

Chapter 6

The Money Trail

The Koots ran as fast as they could. They got to the gas station too late. The police car was just leaving.

"We missed them," said Toby. He kicked some dirt with the toe of his shoe.

"It's time for supper, anyway," said Abe. "I have to go."

"Me too," said Ty and Ben.

"Okay, come to my house after you eat," said Gabe. "We'll plan what to do next."

"I'll see what I can find out from Todd at supper," offered Toby.

When Toby got home, Todd was talking to their mom. He told her what had happened at Ms. Ngu's and at the gas station.

Todd made getting clues easy. All Toby had to do was listen.

Later at Gabe's house, Toby gave his report. "Todd told my mom the same thing Gabe heard. At the gas station, the guy didn't know anything.

"The cop said she'd write up a report. It could be that somebody paid for gas with that funny money.

"Mrs. Ngu got it with her change. She gave it to Todd. And nobody spotted it until I tried to spend it at the Stop 'n Shop."

33

Toby continued, "Todd is really mad. He didn't get paid for his work. The police have his twenty. He's going back to Ms. Ngu to see if she'll give him the other twenty that she has."

"So are the police going to try to catch the crook?" asked Ben.

"They're going to look for more funny money," said Toby.

"I think we'd better check this out," said Ty. Everybody agreed.

"Okay," Gabe said. "Let's go over what we know."

He counted on his fingers as he talked.

Number one. It could be Todd.

Number two. It could be Ms. Ngu.

34

Number three. It could be somebody at the gas station.

Number four. It could be somebody who got gas at the gas station.

Or number five. It could be somebody before that.

"That money could have been spent many times before somebody spotted it," Gabe added.

"Officer Gomez didn't think so," Ben reminded him. "He said it was too crisp to have passed through very many hands."

"And Todd didn't do it. I'm sure of that," Toby added. "He just got the money. And we know where it came from."

"I think we'd better spy on Ms. Ngu," said Ben. "We'll see if she acts strange."

"Let's go there right after school tomorrow," suggested Gabe.

Chapter 7

A Plan Backfires

The Koots found a place to spy. They climbed a tree in the backyard of the house next door. From there they could see Ms. Ngu's house. They had a good view of the backyard and part of the front.

The boys settled in the tree. Soon Ms. Ngu came home from work.

Ms. Ngu let her cat out the back door and waved at her neighbor. He was walking toward the tree in his backyard.

"You boys get down from there! Now! You'll break my tree. And you'll break your necks! Go climb your own trees!"

Ms. Ngu's neighbor stood under the tree. He was looking up and yelling at the Koots. Ms. Ngu walked over to him. They stood and looked up into the tree.

The Koots tried to hide. But it was hard. They had been spotted. The leaves were beginning to shake.

"I guess they see us," whispered Ben.

"I guess I'll get down," whispered Abe.

"Maybe they didn't see me," whispered Ty. He was up the highest. "You guys all get down. I'll stay here and spy."

Ty tried to look like a branch. Abe, Ben, Toby, and Gabe climbed down. They walked past the man and Ms. Ngu.

"You. Up in the tree. I see you," shouted the man. "Don't try to hide."

"What's your buddy's name?" the man asked the Koots.

"Ty," said Gabe quietly.

"Come on down, Ty," said the man. "I'm not going away until you come down."

39

Ty didn't move.

"If you don't come down, I'm going to call the police!" the man yelled.

Ty still didn't move. When the man went to use the phone, he'd climb down. Then the Koots could run. But the man just stood there.

Ms. Ngu cupped her hands around her mouth. She yelled up into the tree. "Are you afraid to come down? We can call the fire department. They will bring a ladder."

Of course, Ty wasn't afraid. And he didn't want anyone to think he was. So he came right down.

"Okay, Ty. You and your buddies beat it," said the man. "I don't want to see you in my yard again. And

never climb my tree. Next time, I will call the police."

The Koots left the yard. They walked down the street.

"I guess we can't spy on Ms. Ngu anymore," said Abe.

"Maybe she and that man will forget what we look like in a week or so," said Gabe.

"Too bad we can't be out after dark," said Ty. "That's the best time to spy."

"Tomorrow let's work on the gas station," suggested Ben. The boys agreed to meet after school.

Chapter 8

Getting Nowhere

The next afternoon, the Koots were sitting in the empty lot across from the gas station. Cars went in and out. People got out and pumped gas into their cars. Then they went inside and paid. The Koots couldn't see much from where they were.

"Maybe we can take turns walking past the window," said Ty.

"Yeah, maybe we'll see something," said Abe.

"I'll be first," said Ty.

Minutes later, a car pulled up. A lady got out and put gas into her car. Then she went inside. Ty ran across the street. He walked slowly past the window. He looked inside. The lady came out, got in her car, and drove away. Ty hurried back across the street.

"What did you see?" asked Toby.

"She gave the guy some money. He gave her some change. I couldn't see much."

"Let me try," said Gabe.

Soon another car pulled up. Gabe ran across the street. The man finished pumping gas into his car. Gabe followed the man into the station.

43

The man came out and left. Then Gabe walked out. He ran across the street to the empty lot.

"He paid with a ten," said Gabe.

"Did the money look okay?" asked Ty.

"I guess so," said Gabe. "It looked old."

"What did you do in there?" asked Ben.

"I asked what time it was," said Gabe. He smiled.

"You can use that once," said Ben. "But how often can we ask what time it is?"

"You know what?" said Toby. "We could sit here all day. And we could walk by the window all day. And we could ask what time it is every time

44

someone pays for gas. But we still won't learn anything."

"You're right!" said Abe. "We need a horoscope."

"A what?" asked Ty. He knew his friend often had trouble with the English language.

"You know. A horoscope. The thing you look at stars with," said Abe.

"A horoscope does have something to do with stars," admitted Gabe.

"What do you mean?" asked Abe.

"Abe, Abe, Abe," said Toby, shaking his head. "A horoscope uses the stars to tell the future."

"You mean a telescope," said Ben. "My grandpa has one. He uses it to study the sky."

45

"Would he let you use it?" asked Gabe.

"Are you kidding?" said Ben. "He won't even let me touch it. It sits at his attic window."

"He just lives down the street from me. Do you think he'd let us see it?" asked Gabe.

"I don't think so," said Ben.

"Well, it can't hurt to ask," said Gabe, already heading in that direction.

Chapter 9

The Attic

Ben's grandpa was taking a nap. His grandma said they could go up to the attic and look around. But they could not touch the telescope.

The Koots climbed the stairs. The house was very old. And the attic was dark and scary. It smelled like dust. There was old stuff everywhere.

Ben flipped on the light at the top of the stairs. "The telescope is in that corner," said Ben. He pointed to a small window.

"Grandpa looks at the stars from here. He also watches the planets and comets."

Ty walked over to the telescope. It was pointed in the direction of the gas station.

Ben looked through the lens. He did not touch it with his hands.

"I can see two blocks away," Ben said. "The people look as if they're right here in the attic."

"Can you see the gas station?" asked Abe.

"I don't know. I can't touch the telescope," said Ben.

48

"Let me help you," said Gabe. He picked up an old shirt. He held it in his hands. He walked over to the telescope and moved it a little to the left.

"You're not supposed to touch it," said Abe.

"I'm not," said Gabe. "The shirt is."

"A little more to the left," said Ben.

Gabe kept moving the telescope a little at a time. Soon Ben could see the gas station.

"I can see in the window!" said Ben. "I can see the cash drawer!"

Just then, the Koots heard footsteps coming up the stairs. They moved away from the telescope. Ben picked up a picture album. He opened it.

"So, what are you young koots doing in my attic?" asked Ben's grandpa.

"We're looking at some pictures," said Ben.

50

"Grandma says for you to come downstairs. She's taking some cookies out of the oven," said Grandpa.

He looked around the attic and then at Ben. "You didn't touch my telescope, did you?" he asked.

"No, sir," said Ben.

As they ate the cookies, Ty said to Ben's grandpa, "Your attic is awesome. I've never been in an attic before."

"Me neither," said Abe.

"Me neither," said Toby.

"I have," said Gabe. "We have one. But it doesn't have all that neat stuff in it."

"Would you guys like to go back up?" asked Ben. "I can show you some really great stuff!"

"Sure," said the Koots.

"Is it okay, Grandpa?" asked Ben.

"I guess so," said Grandpa. "Just don't touch my telescope," he warned.

"We won't," promised Ty.

All week the Koots played in the attic after school. They looked at old pictures.

Sometimes Ben's grandpa would come up and look at the pictures with them. He would tell the boys stories. They searched in boxes and trunks. They found some cool stuff.

And when Grandpa wasn't there, they took turns looking through the telescope. But they never touched it.

At least, not with their hands.

Chapter 10

Case Closed

On Saturday, the Koots were back in the attic. They kept finding more and more cool stuff.

But they hadn't seen anything strange at the gas station. Four of the Koots were bored looking through the telescope. There were just too many fun things to do in the attic. But Ty couldn't stop watching the station.

"Look what I found," said Toby. He held up an old army uniform. He put it on over his clothes.

"Atten—shun!" Ben yelled. Toby put his hand to his forehead.

"At ease, soldier," said Ben. Toby put his arms at his sides. He moved his feet apart.

"Hey, there are more uniforms in here," said Ben. "We can play army!"

Everybody came over to look except Ty.

"Wow!" said Abe. "I want to be in the army!"

Just then Ty said, "Call the cops! Quick! Ask for Officer Gomez. Tell him to meet us at the gas station!"

Ben ran down the stairs to call the police.

"What happened?" asked Abe.

"I'll tell you on the way," said Ty. "Let's go."

The boys flew down the stairs and out the door.

A few minutes later, the Koots were at the gas station. A police car pulled up. Officer Gomez got out. Ty asked the officer to come into the gas station with him.

"Look in the cash drawer, officer," Ty said.

The clerk looked puzzled.

Officer Gomez asked the clerk to open the cash drawer.

"Now, look at all the twenty-dollar bills," said Ty.

The clerk took out the twenty-dollar bills. He handed them to Officer Gomez.

"This one is fake," said Officer Gomez. "It's just like the other one."

Officer Gomez turned and looked at Ty. "How did you know it would be here?" the officer asked.

Ty smiled. "I watched the guy who just got off duty. He took it out of his pocket and put it in here. Then he took a good one from the drawer. He put it in his pocket."

"Where were you?" asked Officer Gomez.

"A couple blocks away," said Ty. "I was looking through a telescope."

"But he didn't touch anything," laughed the other Koots.

The boys slapped each other on the back. Another mystery solved!